One Gift Deserves Another

ADAPTED FROM THE BROTHERS GRIMM

BY Joanne Oppenheim • ILLUSTRATED BY Bo Zaunders

DUTTON CHILDREN'S BOOKS
NEW YORK

This story is freely adapted from "The Turnip," by
the Grimms.

Text copyright © 1992 by Joanne Oppenheim
Illustrations copyright © 1992 by Bo Zaunders

Library of Congress Cataloging-in-Publication Data

Oppenheim, Joanne.
   One gift deserves another/written by Joanne Oppenheim;
illustrated by Bo Zaunders.
      p. cm.
   Summary: When a poor but generous man gives the
king his giant turnip and is richly rewarded, the man's rich,
selfish brother decides to follow suit.
   ISBN 0-525-44975-2
   [1. Generosity—Fiction.   2. Gifts—Fiction.
3. Brothers—Fiction.]   I. Zaunders, Bo, ill.   II. Title.
PZ7.06160n   1992
[E]—dc20   91-46073   CIP   AC

Published in the United States 1992 by
Dutton Children's Books,
a division of Penguin Books USA Inc.
375 Hudson Street, New York, New York 10014

Designer: Joseph Rutt

Printed in Hong Kong   First edition
10 9 8 7 6 5 4 3 2 1

To Donna
my editor and friend
—J.O.

To Roxie
—B.Z.

Once upon a time there were two brothers. One was rich, the other was not.

The rich brother lived in a house that was like a palace. He had a sack full of silver and gold, and his wife wore splendid jewels. In fact, they had everything one could wish for in this world. But the rich brother was a greedy sort. He shared nothing with his brother.

The poor brother and his wife lived in a ramshackle shack. They were poor as poor could be and owned little but the clothes on their backs. From sun up to sun down they worked in their garden, planting seeds and pulling weeds. But what they managed to grow, they shared with their neighbors.

One day as the poor brother was hoeing his garden he came upon a huge mound of earth.

"What's this?" he muttered.

He scratched the soil away and discovered what appeared to be the top of a turnip—except that he had never seen a turnip top so large.

"How wonderful!" said his wife when she saw the turnip top. "This winter we shall have plenty of turnip stew."

And with this happy thought they went back to their chores, working long and hard as usual.

By evening the poor brother and his wife were so
weary they could only eat their meager supper and fall
into bed. They were too tired to notice how much
the turnip in their garden had grown in just one day.

But the next morning, when the poor brother opened the rickety shutters he could not believe his eyes. He thought he must be dreaming.

"Wife! Wife!" he yelled. "Do you see what I see?"

Indeed she did. There in the garden was the enormous turnip, bursting through the earth.

"What in the world can we do with such a turnip?" the wife asked as they admired it from all sides.

"I know!" said the poor but generous brother. "We could invite all of our neighbors for a feast. This turnip will feed at least a hundred people."

"You expect to make a feast out of only a turnip?" exclaimed the wife. "Some feast that would be!"

By evening the turnip had grown still more.

"It's gigantic!" marveled the wife. "But what can we do with it?"

"If I could take it to market," said the poor brother, "I could sell it."

"True," said his wife, "but how would you get it there? You would need a huge wagon with a team of horses, and we have neither."

Just then the rich brother and his wife came riding by.

"Whoa!" cried the greedy brother when he saw the enormous turnip.

"What's this purple mountain?" demanded his wife.

"That's no mountain," answered the poor brother. "That's a turnip. Amazing, isn't it?"

"Ask him," the poor wife whispered to her husband. "Maybe he will loan you a wagon."

So the poor brother asked, although he knew his selfish brother would give him no help.

"Impossible!" replied the rich brother. "I have neither wagon nor horses to spare."

"A poor man like you should grow small turnips," scoffed the rich brother's wife.

And with that, the two of them rode away.

Before long, word spread throughout the
land about the stupendous turnip. People
from every town and village came to see it.
They came by foot,
    by horse,
        by cart,
           and by wagon.
                And late one afternoon...

a gilded carriage pulled by four
white horses arrived.

"The king!" someone shouted.

"It is!" another cried. "It's the king!"

"Make way for the king!"

"Your Majesty!" the poor brother said as he bowed.

"Your Highness!" the poor wife said as she curtsied.

"My, my, my!" the king said as he walked around the turnip. "How round! How perfectly formed! Such a splendid color! What a luscious smell!"

"Since you like it so, sire, it is yours!" said the poor brother.

"Mine? You mean…you would give it to me?"

"This turnip is fit for a king," replied the poor brother. "Take it. It is yours. A gift."

"You are a generous man," said the king. He ordered his men to load the gigantic turnip onto a wagon. Then he turned to the poor brother and his wife.

"My good man," said the king, "one gift deserves another."

And with that he made the poor brother and his wife richer than they ever dreamed. He gave them a chest of gold, and he promised them a vast farm, a fine house, and a splendid coach pulled by four sleek black horses.

When the rich brother heard
how wealthy his poor brother
had become, he was green
with envy.

"If the king gives such gifts for just a turnip," he said
to his wife, "imagine what he would give us
in exchange for my golden candelabra, your jewels,
and our sack of silver and gold!"

"How clever you are!" the rich wife agreed happily.
So the greedy brother invited the king to dinner. He
ordered his cooks to prepare a royal feast.

"Delicious!" the king said after the first course. "Scrumptious!" he said after the second and third. "Delectable!" he sighed after the fourth and fifth. By the time they had finished the twelfth and final course, the king could hardly speak.

"My, my, my!" he belched. "Simply marvelous."

"Your Majesty," the rich brother began. "My wife and I are so honored to have you as a guest, we want to give you a very special gift." Saying this, he presented the king with his prized golden candelabra and the sack of silver and gold. His wife handed the king a velvet-lined box stuffed with all her jewels.

"My, my, my!" gasped the king. "Such beautiful gems! And so much silver and gold! How generous you are!"

"They are yours, sire," said the rich brother.

"In that case," said the king, "one gift deserves another."

The rich brother and his wife smiled. Their plan had worked. They waited eagerly to hear what wonderful gift the king would give them.

"Now let me think," he mused. "What shall I give to you? How will I ever repay your generosity?

"I know! I know exactly what I shall give you! I will return with it tomorrow."

That night the rich brother and his wife could hardly sleep.

"Tomorrow," said the greedy brother, "we will be the richest people in the kingdom."

The next morning a loud thud woke the rich brother and his wife. They jumped out of bed and rushed to the door.

There was the king in his gilded carriage. And there on their very grand front lawn sat the enormous turnip.

"For you," said the king. "This is my gift to you—a treasure beyond compare."

The rich brother and his wife were speechless. Tears rolled down their cheeks.

And so the rich brother ended up owning little more than a giant turnip, while the poor brother and his wife never needed anything again.

In fact, they had so much that they sent the once-rich brother and his wife meat and bread— to go with their turnip.